P9-BJX-446

The WEREWOLF CLUB

#5

The
WEREWOLF CLUB

Meets Oliver Twit

DANIEL AND JILL PINKWATER

ALADDIN PAPERBACKS
New York London Toronto Sydney Singapore

First Aladdin Paperbacks edition February 2002

ALADDIN PAPERBACKS
An imprint of Simon & Schuster
Children's Publishing Division
1230 Avenue of the Americas
New York, NY 10020

Book design by Corinne Allen
The text for this book was set in Weidemann Book.
The illustrations were rendered in Magic Marker,
pen, and imported European wolf spit.

Printed in the United States of America

10 9 8 7 6 5 4 3 2 1

CIP data for this book is available from the Library of Congress.

ISBN 0-689-84571-5

CHAPTER ONE

The Watson Elementary School Werewolf Club sat at its usual table in Honest Tom's Tibetan-American Lunchroom. We were watching Billy Furball lick his plate. We were depressed.

"Did you have to order that disgusting thing?" Lucy Fang asked, sipping her water.

"He who pays, picks," Billy Furball said. "Club rules."

"You *never* ask what anyone else might want," said Henry Count Dorkula.

"And you're not a werewolf, bat boy." Billy burped loudly. "That was yummy."

"Has anyone else ever ordered one of those here?" Ralph Alfa asked. "The Jitterbug, or open-

1

faced mashed potato, meatloaf, and gravy sandwich is not everyone's cup of goop."

"We just added it this week. We must now wait and see if it's popular. More water, folks?" The glamorous Carla Lola Carolina, counterwoman and waitress, filled our glasses.

"If you'd gotten a couple of hot dogs, we all could be eating," I, Norman Gnormal, said.

"I offered you forks for sharing," Billy said, licking his fingers.

"Share that goop? Gooey gravy and mashed potatoes? I might still throw up." Henry Count Dorkula pulled his cape out of harm's way as Billy Furball began licking spilled gravy off the table.

"Little boys and girl of the night, I have an announcement." Mr. Talbot, our faculty advisor, lurched up to our table.

"So announce!" said Lucy Fang.

"I have to go to England," he announced.

"I'll go with you," Billy Furball said.

"Why?" Lucy Fang asked.

"Because I want to," Billy Furball said.

"Not you, slob face. Why does Mr. Talbot have to go to England?"

"I must see about my Uncle Bill's will."

3

CHAPTER TWO

"Your Uncle Bill died?" I asked.

"In 1904. He was my great-uncle," Mr. Talbot said.

"Isn't it a little late to see about his will?" Lucy Fang asked.

"Things move slower abroad," Mr. Talbot said.

"A broad what?" Billy Furball asked.

"Broad? Like a chick, like a dame, like a girl?" Henry Count Dorkula asked.

"Woman, mini-brain." Lucy Fang said. "Not 'girl' or 'chick' or 'dame.'"

"They move slower when they're wide?" Ralf Alfa asked.

"*Abroad.* As in overseas. Over the water. Away from the United States," Mr. Talbot explained.

"I'm going with you!" Billy Furball was bouncing up and down in his chair.

"What's with you, Billy?" Ralf Alfa asked.

"I want to see the royalty. In person."

"But you hate royalty. You're an antimonarchist," said Lucy Fang.

"Right. I'm going to stand outside Buckingham Palace and boo them. Maybe I'll throw rotten tomatoes."

"Let's all go," said Ralf Alfa.

"And how exactly do you propose to pay for your tickets?" asked Mr. Talbot. "I notice you're sitting here drinking water and eating nothing."

"Maybe you'd be willing to extend us a small loan," Henry suggested.

"Come to think of it, I don't have enough money for my own ticket," Mr. Talbot said.

CHAPTER THREE

"Let's forget the whole thing," Mr. Talbot said. "Unless . . ."

"Unless what?" Lucy Fang asked.

"I might have a way for us all to go to England."

"All?" we all asked.

"All! Uncle H. G. Talbot's time-and-space machine! I think it's in the basement."

"Time-and-space machine?"

"Yes. I'm sure it works," Mr. Talbot said. "Well, pretty sure. All we need are 212 double-A batteries and some dustcloths. Old towels will do fine."

"You have an Uncle H. G. who has a time-and-space machine?" I asked.

"What do you mean 'pretty sure'?" asked Lucy Fang.

CHAPTER FOUR

Mr. Talbot's basement was dark and damp and crammed full of old furniture, broken exercise equipment, and what looked and smelled like piles of old laundry.

"Gross," said Lucy Fang, holding her nose.

"There it is, under the trampoline," Mr. Talbot pointed.

"It's too small. We'll never all fit."

"It inflates, I think." Mr. Talbot lifted the trampoline and a couple of bent golf clubs off the time-and-space machine. "Help me get it out of here. It's heavy."

"He thinks it inflates."

"Like a life raft," Mr. Talbot said.

"He thinks it inflates like a life raft. A time-and-

7

space machine. Right."

"Follow me, werewolves." Mr. Talbot kicked aside a couple of large boxes and shouldered a chest of drawers out of the way. He opened a door to his yard.

"Oh goody, we don't have to haul this thing upstairs," Norman Gnormal said.

"Why isn't he helping us? He's at least twice our size," Billy Furball whined.

"Shut up and lift your corner," Ralf Alfa said.

"What corner? There are no corners," Lucy Fang said.

"Just lift," Mr. Talbot said.

"Stop bossing everyone," we all said.

We lifted and dragged and slid H. G. Talbot's time-and-space machine into the yard. Then we stood back and stared at it.

"Beautiful," said Mr. Talbot.

"It looks like a lump of old, mildewed canvas," I said.

"With an Exercycle attached to it," Ralf Alfa said.

"It smells like something died in it," Billy Furball said.

"It's a joke, right, Mr. Talbot?" Henry asked.

"He never jokes," Lucy Fang said.

"Then it's dangerous," Henry said.

"Nonsense. All it needs is a light dusting. And of course it must be inflated." Mr. Talbot pointed to a tube sticking out of the canvas. "Start blowing. Take turns. It shouldn't take very long."

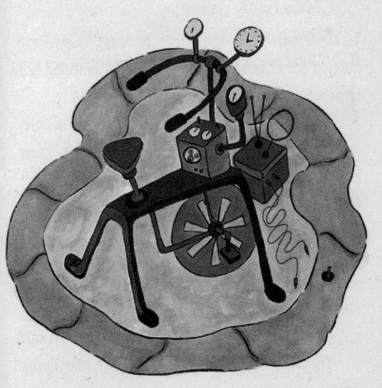

CHAPTER FIVE

"I can't blow out one more breath." Lucy Fang flopped onto her back and gasped what sounded like her last.

Ralf Alfa was taking his turn at inflating the time-and-space machine. He stopped and stuck his finger in the tube. "I think it's full," he announced. "Where's the plug?"

"Plug? Oh yes. Must have been lost," Mr. Talbot said. "I think it needs more inflating. Not quite time for the plug."

"How about you take a turn, Mr. Talbot," Ralf Alfa said.

"He's right. The rest of us have been injuring our lungs for more than an hour," I complained.

"While you've been doing nothing," Henry added.

"*Nothing?* I've been thinking. Planning. Figuring things out. Never mind." Mr. Talbot poked the inflated time-and-space machine. "It appears to be ready. Get the dust rags."

"How about my finger?" Ralf Alfa asked. "It's turning a funny color."

"Righto," said Mr. Talbot.

"Righto?"

"It's a British expression."

"Like 'tallyho'?"

"More like 'good show.'"

"I'm counting to ten and then I'm taking my finger out of here. One . . ."

"Gum. Anyone have any bubble gum?" Mr. Talbot asked.

"Two . . ."

"Someone else take the lad's place at the tube."

No one volunteered.

"Three . . ."

"I have some *old* gum in my pocket," Billy Furball said.

11

"Start chewing. Soften it up a bit," Mr. Talbot ordered.

"Disgusting. Look, it has lint all over it," Lucy Fang said.

"You are one prissy werewolf," Billy Furball said. "It's a good thing this gum is only half a day old."

"Shut up and chew. I can't feel my finger anymore. Four . . ."

CHAPTER SIX

Ralf Alfa had just counted to nine when Billy Furball took the gum out of his mouth.

"It's ready."

"Give it to me." Mr. Talbot pulled Ralf Alfa's finger out of the tube and jammed in the gum. He stuck his ear to the tube. "No leakage. We're just about ready to travel."

"It looks like a life raft . . ."

". . . with an Exercycle in the middle of it . . ."

". . . and weight pulleys like you see on those exercise machines on television . . ."

"And that looks like part of one of the abdomen-buster machines they sell on television . . ."

"And aren't those levers made out of small dumbbells?"

"Your point?" Mr. Talbot asked.

"How does it work?"

"Better yet, does it work?"

"By work do you mean carry passengers through time and space to a specific destination?" Mr. Talbot handed each of us a piece of torn-up towel. "Begin dusting."

"Just tell us. How does this thing work?" Lucy Fang insisted.

"How should I know? My uncle H. G. built it. I seem to remember that you aim it for the time/place you want to be and turn it on. Pretty simple."

"Why don't you call your uncle and ask directions?" I suggested.

Mr. Talbot mumbled something.

"What did you say?"

"I think he said his uncle went missing."

"How?"

"How, Mr. Talbot?"

"No one knows. One day he was here. The next he was gone. The family is hopeful he'll return."

14

"Hopeful? Did he disappear using this machine?" Henry asked.

"Who knows? Can we please get to dusting. Pay particular attention to the gauges. You don't want them getting stuck in transit."

CHAPTER SEVEN

"I'm not getting in this time/space thing," Lucy Fang said.

"You're in it."

"I'm dusting. I mean to travel. Hey, Mr. Talbot, when this goes, does it get you to where you want to be?"

"By that you mean, is it accurate?"

"That's what I mean."

"Within a couple of minutes, a couple of feet— close enough."

"I'm definitely not going."

"Me either."

"Should I go home and pack?" Billy Furball asked.

"No room for luggage, but it might be wise to take a toothbrush and a sweater. London can get chilly in the evening."

"I'm going home. It's suppertime and I'm starving," Ralf Alfa said.

"Me, too."

"Me, too."

"Folderol and piffle. I'm ringing up your parents and telling them we're going on a club trip. They'll be glad of a chance to shovel out your rooms. We shall clean out my refrigerator and have a feast. I have an abundance of sweaters I can lend you."

"You can't force us to go with you," I said.

"Force? Ridiculous. Coerce, possibly. Are you wusses or werewolves? Have you no sense of adventure? Don't you wish to widen your horizons, gain firsthand knowledge of another part of the world?"

"Wusses? I'm no wuss." Ralf Alfa was the first to take the bait.

"Sounds like you're afraid to go alone," Henry said to Mr. Talbot.

Mr. Talbot said "Harrumph."

"I think nothing is going to happen. Look at that thing. Even the gauges are off old exercise machines. Let's eat, get in, pretend to turn it on, and then go home." I, Norman Gnormal, was very sure of my reasoning.

We ate a huge and strange dinner, cleaning out Mr. Talbot's entire refrigerator, including the old ketchup and mustard, and went back into the yard.

Mr. Talbot showed us where to insert the 212 double-A batteries and we climbed into the time-and-space machine. Mr. Talbot handed each of us an enormous sweater.

"Put them on. I hear it gets cold in the in-between."

"In-between?"

Mr. Talbot pulled a lever. Then another. Then he hit a gauge with his hand. Nothing happened.

"See. I told you. Let's go home," I said.

"Battery's in wrong somewhere. Get out and search," Mr. Talbot said.

We all got out and Mr. Talbot supervised while we checked each of the 212 double-A batteries.

Sure enough, battery number 152 had been put in backward.

Once more we got into the machine. It was pretty crowded, but most of us didn't expect to be in it long. Levers were pulled and pushed. Lucy Fang rolled her eyes. Henry drummed his fingers on the inflated canvas. I yawned.

Suddenly the time-and-space machine moved with a sickening lurch. The Watson Elementary School Werewolf Club screamed.

CHAPTER EIGHT

We were surrounded by a fog so thick that we couldn't see each other.

Mr. Talbot was still screaming when I asked, "Where are we?"

"How should I know? I'm only three inches from you. I guess it's foggy over here, too."

"You don't have to be nasty, Lucy. I was asking Mr. Talbot."

"He can't hear you over his own screaming. How do we get him to shut up? I'm getting a headache," Henry said.

"Mr. Talbot, please stop screaming," Ralf Alfa said.

"Right, that'll work."

"You have a better idea, Lucy?"

"Is he still sitting on the bike?"

"Can't tell. Wait. I can feel his leg. Yes."

"Lean over and bite him. Hard."

"Me?"

"Anyone. We have to get his attention."

"Ooooow! Yipes! Ouch! Stop that." Mr. Talbot stopped screaming. "I said *stop it!*"

"Whoever is biting him, you can stop now," Lucy said.

"Okay," we all answered.

"Where are we, Mr. Talbot?" Lucy asked.

"In Limbo, the in-between place. Traveling through. It's where you go when you're moving in time and space at the same time."

"And we're traveling in both time and space?" I asked.

"Of course. A little of each. Actually, probably more space than time this trip. But we'll wind up in London at the same exact minute we left home."

"You sure of that?" Lucy Fang asked.

Mr. Talbot didn't answer.

CHAPTER NINE

The time-and-space machine lurched again. It seemed to drop onto a hard surface. It bounced a couple of times. The thick, white fog was gone. Now it was dark gray. Almost black.

"Where are we?" we all were mumbling.

"London, of course," Mr. Talbot said.

"How do you know?"

"Why is it still foggy?"

"Why are my eyes burning?"

"Why is this fog gritty?"

"Look at your watches. It's exactly the same time it was when we left," Mr. Talbot said confidently.

"I can't see my watch."

"I didn't look at mine when we left."

"Take my word for it, children of the night."

"Speaking of night, did you pack a flashlight?"

"No need. This fog is probably the end of the time/space limbo cycle. It will lift momentarily and we will go about our business. Be patient."

"He said it again," said Lucy. "Probably."

"So?" said the ever-loyal Billy Furball. "We're in England and it didn't cost us a dime to get here."

"We don't know where we are."

"Wherever it is, it stinks. Kind of like a combination of a sewer, a decaying swamp, and something awful burning," observed Henry.

We sat silently for a while. The fog did not lift as promised.

"Let's just go home," I suggested. "How about it, Mr. Talbot."

Mr. Talbot didn't answer.

"Mr. Talbot!" I shouted. *"Did you hear me?"* I admit, I was panicking.

Mr. Talbot muttered something under his breath.

"What? What did you say?"

Henry's bat ears had heard the mumblings of our

leader. "He said we can't go home. Yet. The batteries he used were very old. They don't have enough juice in them. We have to find a store and buy new ones. No problem."

"*No problem?* We can't see a foot in front of us. We have no idea where we are. And does he even have the money to buy 212 double-A batteries?"

"I have a credit card," Mr. Talbot said. "Now relax until we can see."

CHAPTER TEN

We didn't exactly relax, but we waited. We had no choice. After a long while, it did begin to get a little lighter. The air was still kind of black and thick, but we could see, sort of. We were on a roof. We got out of the machine and looked over the edge. The building was only four stories high. There were other small buildings in all directions. They all had chimneys. Black sooty smoke poured out of every one of them.

"That explains the air."

"Isn't that the sun coming up? Exact same time as we left? Hah!"

"London time," Mr. Talbot explained. "You have to adjust for time zones. It was the exact same time back home."

"He's starting to rant."

"What's that down there? In the street?"

"Looks like a horse and carriage. London sure is quaint."

"How about over there?"

"A couple of more horses and carts."

Lucy was leaning over the back of the building. "There're little buildings behind most of the houses. They look like small stables. Some look like out-houses. It's like a picture in my history book."

"Don't dawdle. Follow me," Mr. Talbot instructed. "We should be on our way. The sooner we find the solicitors, the sooner we conduct our business and buy the batteries."

"Solicitors?"

"Lawyers."

We followed Mr. Talbot through a roof door, down four flights of stairs, and into the street. We heard noises behind apartment doors but met no one in the hallways. It was very early in the morning in London.

"*Pee-eww*. The stink is worse down here than on the roof."

"How come none of the buildings have fire escapes?"

"How come there are no cars parked on the street?"

"How come there's a guy over there turning off the streetlights one by one?"

"How come there are all these piles of horse poop in the street?"

"How come that man over there is wearing those strange clothes?"

"Don't mention to anyone in London that you're werewolves. They have stricter rules over here than at home," Mr. Talbot said, marching down the sidewalk toward the streetlight man.

"My good man, would you mind telling me what year this is?"

"You pulling my leg, guv? Or maybe you had a bit too much to drink. Now be a good fellow and take the kiddies home and sleep it off."

"Humor me, fellow. The year?" Mr. Talbot said.

"1890, of course. Now get about your business."

We kiddies were in a whole lot of trouble.

CHAPTER ELEVEN

"We're toast."

"Eighteen ninety? Did they make batteries in 1890?"

"I'm starving. Can we get some food?"

"How? We don't have money. Especially 1890 English money."

"Mr. Talbot has a credit card."

"Great. Let's find an 1890 cash machine."

"What we are going to find is my Uncle Bill. He will help us."

"But he's dead."

"He's dead in the year 2001, not in the year 1890. He lived in quite a nice neighborhood. On some square or other. We'll ask directions."

There must be a million squares in London. We were hopelessly lost and practically fainting from hunger when Henry grabbed a small, dirty kid by the arm.

"What are you doing, Henry?"

"Keeping this jerk's fingers out of my pocket."

"Hey, let go!"

"No way, thief."

"I didn't get anything," the kid whined.

"That's because I don't have anything."

"None of you had anything."

"You were in all our pockets?"

"So what?"

"A genuine pickpocket, neat."

"I have my skills."

"You have a name?"

"What's it to you?"

"Mine's Lucy Fang."

"Oliver Twit. You folks aren't from around here, are you?

"Not hardly."

CHAPTER TWELVE

Oliver Twit knew where just about every rich person in London lived.

"I like to spread myself out a bit. You know, never pick the same pocket twice in the same month. You don't want them recognizing you. Except when you're sticking your hand out and not pinching, of course."

"Huh?" said Ralf Alfa.

"Sometimes he picks pockets. Sometimes he begs," Lucy explained.

"Begs?"

"Is he quite all there?" Oliver Twit asked, jerking his thumb at Ralf Alfa.

"His brain is slowing down from hunger," I said.

"Wait here." Oliver Twit said, waving at some benches in a little park.

In no time at all he was back with a bagful of hot rolls.

We ate while he talked. "Faces are kind of my hobby. Putting them to names, that is. Some of these gents are right generous, specially if you mention them by name . . . Sir this, Mister that. They see me on the street looking tattered and torn and they stick a penny or two in my hand. Your look-alike relative gave me half a crown the last time he seen me. Lord William did."

"A penny or two?" asked Billy Furball.

"It's 1890, nit. A penny buys more," said Lucy Fang.

"Mr. Talbot's uncle is a lord?"

"Maybe it's a different William Talbot."

"Looks just like him," Oliver Twit said, pointing at Mr. Talbot. "I'll show you."

In no time at all we were on a beautiful street. All the houses were large and faced a little fenced park. Mr. Talbot walked up the wide, brick steps and took

hold of the brass knocker attached to the door. He made a terrible racket banging it against the polished wood.

"May I help you?" The tall man in a black suit sounded annoyed. Then he took a close look at us. "No riff-raff allowed here. Go away." He backed into the house.

Mr. Talbot stuck his foot in the door. "Please tell my uncle that his nephew Lawrence is here to see him."

"A likely story." The man slammed the door on Mr. Talbot's foot.

CHAPTER THIRTEEN

We sat on the steps and waited.

The man in black came back.

"Urchins and adult ragamuffin, my master will see you, although I have no idea why."

"He's the butler, isn't he?" Ralf whispered.

"No, he's the king of England," said Henry.

"What do you know about butlers, fruit bat?" I asked.

"More than you, dog boy."

"Wolf."

"Shut up. You know what Mr. Talbot said about English customs being different from ours," Lucy Fang warned.

"What are you people talking about?" Oliver

Twit asked.

"Nothing," we all answered.

The butler led us into a large, high-ceilinged room that was lined with books.

"Wait here and don't touch anything," he sniffed at us.

"Come now, Simms, these are our guests. Now which one of you claims to be my nephew?"

A man, who could have been Mr. Talbot's double had he been thirty or forty years younger, walked into the room.

"Don't they have mirrors in 1890?" Lucy Fang asked.

"Shh."

Mr. Talbot rushed forward and threw his arms around Lord William Talbot. "Uncle Bill!" he shouted.

"Unhand me, ruffian." Uncle Bill stepped back, stared at Mr. Talbot and then said, "You look nothing like your mother."

CHAPTER FOURTEEN

"My mother? You know my mother?" Mr. Talbot asked.

"I think I do. Your mother, my brother's wife. You said you are my nephew," Uncle Bill said.

"I look like my father. All the Talbot men look alike."

"True. Pity. How is your mother?"

"Well, you don't actually know *my* mother."

"Of course I do. We had tea just last Tuesday," Uncle Bill said.

"No, you don't. You see, you're not exactly my regular uncle. . . . I'm not exactly your immediate nephew . . . the son of your brother."

"I knew it," shouted Simms, the butler.

"No, listen. We are related. You're my great-great-uncle. I'm your real nephew . . . but from the future . . . from the United States of America. . . ." Mr. Talbot started to sound desperate.

"Lunatics. I'll get an officer of the law," Simms said, leaving the room.

"Daft," said Oliver Twit.

"True," said Lucy Fang.

"True?"

"Absolutely."

"Those shoes you're wearing weren't made in London," Oliver Twit said.

"They won't be made for more than a hundred years," Billy Furball said.

"Wish to barter?" said Oliver Twit.

"What do you have?"

Oliver Twit picked up a small silver statue of a horse. "This."

"You can't barter something you just stole."

"I don't see why not." Oliver Twit looked disappointed. He slipped the horse into his pocket.

"Put that back, urchin, or no more half crowns from me. This entire business is nonsense," said Uncle Bill.

"Please listen. We're from the future. Got here in a time-and-space machine. Came to see your solicitors, Smith, Peabody, and Cuthbert about your will," said Mr. Talbot.

"Hah! My solicitors are Smith, Smith, and Smith. You are an imposter, false nephew."

"Apparently the Smiths were bought out by the

other guys. I'm your real nephew. I'm your descendent," Mr. Talbot said.

"And I'm the king of Switzerland."

"Do you know the queen?" Billy Furball asked.

"What?"

"We really are from the future," Lucy Fang said.

"What's more," said Ralf Alfa before anyone could stop him, "we're werewolves. Except for him. Henry Count Dorkula is a vampire—sort of."

"The young man is a count? That makes all the difference in the world," said Uncle Bill, Lord Talbot. "The aristocracy does not lie. Are you from the future, young count?"

"Yep," said Henry. "May I use your bathroom?"

CHAPTER FIFTEEN

"You wish to bathe?"

"No, I wish to pee."

"Me, too."

"Me, too."

"Then why on earth did you ask for the bathroom? Simms will show you to the water closet. You are lucky. We are one of the first homes in this city to have indoor facilities.

"Simms, stop lurking outside the door and escort these children. Watch the small, dirty one. He steals."

As she left the room, Lucy asked, "How come you didn't blink an eye when Ralf Alfa mentioned we were werewolves."

41

"It was the one piece of information that convinced me you are who you say you are."

"It was? I thought you were convinced because you think Henry Count Dorkula is a count."

"He's not a count?"

"Count is his middle name."

"It is *not*," said Henry. "I'm a real count—a Romanian one!"

"No matter," said Uncle Bill. This Ralf Alfa lad is privy to a closely guarded Talbot family secret."

"He is? Ralf Alfa is privy to something?"

"What's 'privy'?" Ralf Alfa asked.

"It means you know something."

"I know? What?"

"The Talbot men have always been werewolves," said Uncle Bill.

"I know that?"

"All of them?"

"All."

"How? Is it genetic?"

"Genetic? What does that mean? There is a saying in our family, 'When the moon is bright, you take a bite, and make your little boy a creature of the night.' It's a Talbot family tradition—biting the hand of the male child you feed. It's how we pass on our gift to the next generation."

CHAPTER SIXTEEN

We were starving hungry. Lord William Talbot had his cook prepare a huge meal for us. While we sampled the exotic food of England, we asked questions about London in 1890. The first thing we learned was that the entire city stank. All the time. Lord Talbot explained that between the outhouses, the sewers that emptied into the river, the general lack of bathing facilities, the horse waste, the burning of garbage, and the use of coal fires to heat the houses, stink was a way of life. So was poverty. Oliver Twit, who was twelve, lived on the streets along with thousands of other kids.

"But me, I'm a lucky 'un. I got fast fingers an' a winning smile. Right, guv?" Oliver Twit explained as he stuffed a forkful of jellied eel into his mouth.

"Those fast fingers are going to land you straight in prison one of these days," Lord Talbot scolded.

Oliver scooped up some bangers and mash—sausage and potatoes. "Maybe, but now I'm not starving. Besides, I never takes what a poor man needs."

"I *love* this food," Billy Furball announced. "I can't wait to eat some genuine London fish and chips. Is that treacle pudding? This eel goo is just great! I could eat this stuff forever."

"You might be doing just that," said Lucy Fang, moving her food from one side of her plate to the other. "I don't think they made double-A batteries in 1890. I think we're stuck here—forever."

"No!" all the werewolves said and looked at Mr. Talbot.

Mr. Talbot stared at his plate.

CHAPTER SEVENTEEN

"You can all live here with me. You can call me Uncle Bill and we can run together when the moon is full."

"That's very generous, Uncle Bill. But I must get these youngsters home." Mr. Talbot looked miserable.

"I think I know just the bloke to help you, guv." Oliver said. "Smart chap. People just naturally knock on his door when they need figuring out done right."

"Aha. Do you mean . . . ," began Uncle Bill.

"Yes, sir. I run an errand for him now and then . . . I keep an ear to the ground in certain circles where no one notices a lad like me. Pays handsomely, he does."

"What are they talking about?" Ralf Alfa asked.

"Who, Ralf, not what," Henry corrected.

"The man in question is the great detective . . . ," Oliver began.

"Sherlock Holmes!" everyone but Ralf Alfa said.

"Right. How do you folks know his name if you're from the future?"

"We'll explain on the way. Can you take us to 221B Baker Street immediately?" Mr. Talbot said.

"His address? You know that, too?"

"How far is it? It's pretty late."

"Mr. Holmes is up till all hours of the night, but it's miles from here," Oliver Twit said.

"Take my carriage. In fact, I'll accompany you. Simms, have the stableman harness the horses."

In minutes we were on our way. Even with two of us sitting on top with the coachman, the inside of the carriage was crowded—and ripe. We had begun to smell like the rest of London.

CHAPTER EIGHTEEN

We werewolves were pretty exhausted but the carriage ride through the cobbled streets was way too rough for us to nap. We pulled up in front of a brick house. As we stepped onto the street, I looked up. The windows on the top floor were lit. A man looked down at us and then moved back into the room. "I can't believe we're going to meet Sherlock Holmes," Lucy Fang said. "He's the smartest man in London except maybe for his brother, Mycroft."

"You know that, too?" Oliver said and pulled the bell cord next to the door.

"We explained it all to you on the way over here."

"Still, it boggles the mind."

"Boggle or not, isn't that bell going to wake the

whole rooming house?"

"Mr. Holmes and the doctor are the only ones who have rooms here and the landlady ignores callers this time of night."

A shortish man with a large mustache opened the door. "I am Dr. Watson," he announced. "Please follow me."

We followed him up the stairway to the top floor. Then we were inside the great detective's apartment—or rooms, as they were called in London. We gawked at everything—the gaslights on the wall, the old-fashioned scientific equipment on a table, the knickknacks, the furniture, and, mostly, the tall, big-nosed man in a smoking jacket who was leaning against the fireplace mantle and puffing on a pipe. He was holding a magnifying glass in his hand and staring at us as if we were a bunch of strange bugs that had crawled in.

None of us seemed to be able to speak. Except Oliver. "Mr. Holmes . . . ," he began.

"Shhhh," said the great detective and closed the distance between us.

CHAPTER NINETEEN

Mr. Talbot stuck out his hand. "It is a pleasure . . . ," he began.

"Shhh . . . ," said Sherlock Holmes, plucking something off Mr. Talbot's jacket.

Sherlock Homes walked slowly past each club member, staring each of us in the face. He looked at our clothing through his magnifying glass and knelt down for a few seconds and touched Lucy Fang's shoes. When he got to Henry, he ran his finger over the lapel of Henry's cape, sniffed it, and then touched it to his tongue.

"I bet he won't do that with Billy Furball," I whispered to Lucy Fang.

"Shhhh . . . ," said the great detective, walking

back to the fireplace.

"So, now it is up to me to deduce why four juvenile and two adult werewolves, and one juvenile fruit vampire have paid me a visit in the middle of the night. . . ."

"Well . . . ," began Lord William Talbot.

Sherlock Holmes held up a hand. "Obviously, the two adult werewolves are related, although the older is a member of the aristocracy and the younger is certainly not from London, or England, or, most likely, from this period of time."

We were stunned into silence.

Sherlock Holmes continued. "The clothing you are wearing bears no resemblance to clothing worn in this part of the world, and the fabric is nothing yet known on Earth. This holds true for the shoes on your feet. Quite remarkable. So, I deduce, you are, with the exception of young Oliver and this gentleman, Lord William Talbot, from some time in the future."

"I say, Holmes. Very good, indeed," Dr. Watson said. "But werewolves and a fruit vampire?"

"The long wolf hairs found on the clothing were an obvious clue . . . also a slight cast of the eyes and a distinctive odor."

"We smell?" Lucy Fang was upset. "Probably because we've been in stinky London for too long."

"It's not an offensive odor, and in all probability it's undetectable to the ordinary, untrained nose. I will continue. The young fruitpire resembles his ancestor, the cause of the last great outbreak of scurvy in London, the most horrible Noshferatu. . . ."

"My great-great-great-great uncle . . . ," Henry said.

". . . In addition, his cape is stained with fruit juice in several places . . . and his ears are as pointy as a bat's. Furthermore, I deduce you have come here to ask for my help in transporting yourselves to your place in the future. Has your means of transportation been lost or broken? No, wait. I'll tell you. It is not working."

"You are a genius," we all said.

"Of course," said the great detective.

CHAPTER TWENTY

"Of course I will help you . . . if you agree to certain conditions," said the great Holmes.

"There are conditions?"

"Ones that are not without interest. You, furry creatures of the night, are going to help me rid London of one of its most notorious criminals."

"We are?"

"You are."

"And this criminal?"

"A monster. Jack the Schlepper." Sherlock Holmes began pacing back and forth. "Jack the Schlepper is a man of superhuman strength. He is able to carry an entire houseful of loot in a sack on his back . . . and outrun the constabulary while doing so.

"He is a fiend who shows no mercy to anyone who tries to apprehend him. He has tossed pursuers into the river, stuffed them into trunks, and hung them by their heels from London Bridge. I, myself, have had my hands on Jack no less than four times. During three of those scuffles, I was being assisted by no fewer than twenty policeman. And yet Jack the Schlepper escaped my grasp. You are the last hope of the decent citizens of London."

"Are these decent citizens friendly to were-wolves?" I asked.

"We will not inform anyone you are on the case," Sherlock Holmes said. "Tomorrow night, at the Tower of London, we will have Jack the Schlepper in chains."

"Why the Tower of London?" Mr. Talbot asked.

"Jack the Schlepper is planning to steal the crown jewels of England. They are kept in the Tower."

"How do you know his plans, Mr. Holmes?" Billy Furball asked.

Holmes withdrew a letter from his inside pocket. "The rascal has had the nerve to send me a letter."

Holmes read:

"Dear Mr. Holmes, I hope this finds you well and also Dr. Watson and your cat and Mrs. Hudson, your Scottish landlady. I am going to steal the crown jewels soon, and there is nothing you can do to stop me. Nyah, nyah, nyah, nyah, nyah! Your friend, Jack the Schlepper."

"This is shocking, Mr. Holmes," Lord William Talbot said.

"Not only is he an awful criminal, but you see what a monkey he is—sending me letters and saying he is my friend. He is mocking me, but I will get the better of him tonight," said Sherlock Holmes.

"We can do this. We're stronger than strong— when we're in the werewolf mode. And there are six of us," Lord William Talbot insisted.

"Do we have a choice?" his nephew asked.

"Not if you want my help in getting you home," Sherlock Holmes answered.

"But we can't just become werewolves because we have a job to do. We need a full moon," I explained.

"Then this coming night will be perfect."

We looked out the window into the sooty darkness.

"How can you tell?" Lucy Fang asked.

"I am Sherlock Holmes. I know things. Go to Lord William Talbot's house. Rest. Eat. I will meet you there at precisely nine o'clock this evening. Together we shall storm the Tower of London and save the crown jewels."

"But how do you know Jack the Schlepper is going to commit the crime tonight?"

"I know things. I have my methods."

CHAPTER TWENTY-ONE

On the way back to Lord William Talbot's house, it dawned on us. We were going to raid the Tower of London, the place where throughout history, prisoners were held and tortured and beheaded. We were supposed to keep Jack the Schlepper, the strongest bad man in London, from stealing the crown jewels—without letting anyone know we were werewolves.

"Do they still do those things to people in the tower?"

"How do I know?"

"Doesn't matter. We're the good guys."

"If anyone sees us running around as werewolves, they won't think that."

"Mr. Holmes will protect us."

"You think?"

"What if this Schlepper person is stronger than us?"

"What if he's not human?"

"Then we can eat him."

"That's your solution to all problems, Billy Furball."

"So?"

When we got back to his house, Uncle Bill insisted all the kids take baths before getting into clean beds. Oliver said he didn't want to bathe. Hadn't done so in maybe a year, but Uncle Bill said no bath, no more half crowns. We were getting used to calling Lord William Talbot Uncle Bill. He gave us all nightshirts, and the now clean time travelers fell asleep around four in the morning.

CHAPTER TWENTY-TWO

We stumbled out of bed at noon. We hung around the house in our nightshirts because Uncle Bill had had our clothing washed. It was hanging on a line in back of his house getting sooty.

"Didn't anyone tell him that our clothing gets torn and ruined when we become werewolves?" Lucy asked.

"Figured he knew that, being one himself."

"Still, it'll be nice wearing clean stuff for a few hours."

"Clean?"

"Well, not smelly."

"Our clothes are out there hanging in the air, aren't they? The stinky, foggy, sooty air you can

60

see. *And* they were washed in London water . . ."

"You're pretty grouchy, Lucy," Ralf Alfa said.

"Well, I happen to like my family *and* my life and I'm just a little put out that I'll *never see anyone or anything I like again!*" Lucy screeched at us and stomped off to sulk.

We spent the rest of the day asking questions about the year 1890. Uncle Bill told us we were in Victorian England—named after Queen Victoria who had been ruling for years and years.

"Think I'll get to see her?" Billy Furball had spent part of the afternoon trying to organize the servants to start a revolution. They had ignored him.

"Not if you're going to lob a rotten fruit at her head," Oliver Twit said.

"You're a royalist?" Billy said. "You, an urchin of the streets who has to beg . . . and even steal in order to live. *You* are defending this Victoria who lives in a palace?"

"She's the queen," Oliver said.

Evening came. We were all relieved when it

was time to get dressed. We looked about as grubby as we had before our clothes were washed. At nine o'clock Sherlock Holmes and Dr. Watson arrived.

CHAPTER TWENTY-THREE

"But they're not werewolves, Holmes," Dr. Watson observed.

"Must be that infernal fog. Well, never mind. There's evil afoot. Follow me, werewolves and fruit-pire."

"But we're not werewolves yet. How can we stop Jack the Schlepper? We're kids. We're small. . . ."

"He's right, Holmes," Uncle Bill said. "It's too dangerous to . . ."

But Sherlock Holmes dragged and pushed us out the door. In minutes we were headed top speed to the Tower of London. None of us felt any werewolfish change coming on.

"What I feel is seasick," said Henry.

The carriage was bouncing and rocking as it bumped its way through the cobbled streets.

"What *is* that smell?" Lucy Fang asked.

"Aha! I knew your wolf senses would emerge. *That* is the river Thames. We are almost at the Tower."

"Nothing is emerging, Mr. Holmes. We're still just kids."

"Maybe we're on moon time from the United States . . . from the twenty-first century," said Mr. Talbot.

"What does that mean?"

"I was simply speculating."

Then it happened. The carriage stopped. We got out. For just a moment the fog parted and we could see the moon in all its roundness. The back of my hands began to itch.

"I'm changing."

"Me, too."

"Me, too."

Soon the members of the Watson Elementary School Werewolf Club plus the two Talbots threw back their heads and howled. Henry flew around our heads making screeching bat noises. We were strong. We were brave. We were werewolves . . . and a fruit-pire.

"Follow me, creatures of the night," Sherlock Holmes said. "According to my calculations, Jack the Schlepper has entered the Tower and is filling his sacks with the treasures of England."

We loped behind Sherlock Holmes to the Tower. The fortified door had been ripped off its hinges.

"Wow," said Ralf Alfa.

"Not too subtle, is he?" said Lucy Fang.

"Shhhh," said Sherlock Holmes.

We crept up some stone steps. Another thick door had been destroyed—smashed to smithereens.

"Oh, boy," someone whispered.

"Now!" Sherlock Holmes shouted as he stepped aside.

"Schlepper, your goose is cooked! You are under arrest."

CHAPTER TWENTY-FOUR

It's possible that Jack the Schlepper was not only the strongest man in London but the strongest man in the history of the world. Also the ugliest . . . and most determined. It took all of us working together to hold him. He kicked, he bit, he tossed us around like rag dolls. He got Mr. Talbot in a headlock that we were sure would be the end of him. We bounced off the walls and back onto Jack the Schlepper. Over and over again. Finally, panting and exhausted, we pinned him to the floor. Sherlock Holmes blew a whistle. A bunch of policemen arrived carrying heavy chains.

They must have been warned about us because never once did any of them look at us. They wrapped Jack the Schlepper in the chains.

"You are on your way to Dartmoor Prison where you will spend the rest of your life, rascal!" Sherlock Holmes said.

"Don't be so fast to think me finished, detective. I will return, and you'll rue this day," Jack the Schlepper threatened.

"Take him away, men," Sherlock Holmes ordered.

The policemen dragged a screaming and cursing Jack the Schlepper out of the Tower of London.

There were huge, bulging sacks and a lot of broken glass on the floor. We wandered around looking at several rooms of empty cases. There wasn't a jeweled crown or necklace in sight.

"May we see the jewels in the sacks?" Mr. Talbot asked.

"Yes, but they aren't the real jewels. When I discovered Jack the Schlepper's plans, I requested that the crown jewels be replaced by copies . . . just in case you had failed to subdue the monster."

"So we risked our lives for nothing?"

"Not for nothing. You risked your lives in the service of the Queen."

"I think I'm going to throw up," said Billy Furball.

"Are you going to tell us how to get home now?" Lucy Fang asked.

"Let us return to Lord William Talbot's house and discuss the matter."

"Uh oh. He hasn't thought of anything," Lucy Fang said.

"Great detective, my foot."

"I knew it, we're stuck here forever."

"Hey, does that mean some of us could be our own ancestors?"

"Oh, ick. Disgusting."

CHAPTER TWENTY-FIVE

By the time we got back to Uncle Bill's house, we were really hungry. The servants had prepared a huge breakfast of English specialties—kippers, sausage, bacon, eggs, toast, potatoes, grilled tomatoes, muffins—and then left to hide in their rooms. It was only about one in the morning. We were still looking like werewolves.

"I have thoroughly researched the item you need to return to your own time and place," Sherlock Holmes began.

"Items," Lucy corrected. "Two hundred twelve of them."

"Quite so. Without boring you with the details, in the year 1799, a man named Alessandro Volta invented the first device that allowed scientists to control the discharge of electricity."

"A battery!" we all said at once. Things were looking up.

And down. "A primitive device. Although Volta was brilliant and invented a number of other devices . . ."

"About the batteries, Mr. Holmes?"

"Ah, yes. Progress has been made, of course, but I fear there is nothing that exists in 1890 that is powerful enough to replace your 212 double-A batteries. . . ."

"I knew it. We're stuck here. My life is ruined." Lucy Fang slumped in her chair and sulked.

"Perhaps not. There might be another means of creating a sufficient surge of power to make the trip."

We all held our breaths while the detective took his time.

"It is still night. This must be attempted while you are in your wolf form. Do you change back to human form at dawn?"

"Usually."

"Then we must move with great haste. I wish that aggravating woman would get here so we could leave."

"What woman? Let's just go."

"We *must* wait. It is protocol. She insisted that you be thanked in person—if the mission were successful."

There was a great banging on the front door. Simms, the only servant not afraid of us, went to see who was there. Four huge men in fancy uniforms marched into the room and stood aside. A small, elderly, round woman in a long black dress strode in behind them. Lord William Talbot and Oliver bowed from their waists.

"Oh wolfspit, it's Queen Victoria," Billy Furball said. "I recognize her from my history book." Billy picked up a muffin.

"Don't you dare throw that!" Mr. Talbot warned.

"Ah, the young antiroyalist. Our special thanks to you, young wolf, for overcoming your feelings and helping to save the crown jewels." Queen Victoria patted Billy Furball on his hairy arm.

"And to all of you for ridding the people of the Empire of a horrible menace. And now we have a surprise for you all. One which will solve your problem of transportation home."

"But ma'am," Sherlock Holmes began.

Queen Victoria ignored him and turned to the door. "You may enter now."

CHAPTER TWENTY-SIX

In walked Mr. Talbot's mother. Or maybe it was her exact double. Then she spoke and we knew.

"Lawrence, you dummkopf, how can one werewolf get into so much trouble in a lifetime?" Mrs. Talbot walked up to Mr. Talbot, stood on tiptoe, and slapped him on the side of his head.

"You always said I was born under an unlucky star, Mommy. Is it really you?"

"No, it's the man in the moon. I came to rescue you and your charges. But first I had to stop and visit my old friend, Victoria Regina."

"It really is you, Mommy."

"Close your mouth, Lawrence. I've brought you 230 double-A batteries fresh in their packages."

"We only need 212," Mr. Talbot stammered.

"If you had had the good sense to take extras with you, you wouldn't be stuck here, would you?" Mommy Talbot asked.

"But Madame," Sherlock Holmes said, "there is no need for your help. I have solved the problem."

"You're a very nice, smart boy, Sherlock, but your solution won't work. It's been tried."

"I beg your pardon, Madame . . . ," the great detective huffed.

"Don't get on your high horse. Want an explanation? Then someone get some comfortable chairs for the Queen and me—and a couple of cups of tea would be nice."

There was a whole lot of rushing around. Soon Victoria, the Queen of England, and Mrs. Talbot, her old friend, were sipping tea and nibbling on cookies.

"It's the middle of the night and we need our rest, so I'll be brief," said Mrs. Talbot. "I'll answer your questions. No, put your hands down. I know what they are.

"First, naturally I got here in my time-and-space machine."

"You have a . . . ," Mr. Talbot began.

"Shut up, lummox, I want to get this over with. I go places in my time-and-space machine at least once a week. It's the updated model—made of hand-tooled parts with modern controls. Not anything like that thing you traveled in. That was one of H. G.'s prototypes. You could have landed anywhere—any time. You could have dumped these children in the middle of an ocean or stranded them forever in pre-historic times. That machine is totally unstable.

"Back to your questions. I was getting ready to take my weekly trip when the energy indicator, which keeps time-and-space machines from crashing into each other, showed there was another machine in motion nearby. This was momentarily confusing because the closest machine I knew of was in France. Then I remembered the prototype and rushed over to your house. I was too late.

"Fortunately, I was able to trace your route. I noticed your old boxes of batteries were empty so I brought along replacements. Once here, I decided to visit my old friend Queen Victoria, whom I met years ago when I was out exploring. That about covers everything."

"It does not, Madame," said Sherlock Holmes.

"Oh right. Your plan. You had figured out that Lawrence, in werewolf form, could peddle a slightly adjusted time-and-space machine with enough force to replace the batteries. Not bad for a man working with so little modern scientific knowledge."

I thought Sherlock Holmes was going to either strangle Mrs. Talbot or explode.

Mrs. Talbot continued. "Peddling the prototype machine at werewolf speed will make it move, but who knows where. H. G. himself was lost for a year wandering through time and space before accidentally finding his way home. He, too, forgot to take along extra batteries, Lawrence. You should have read his diaries. *He* should have re-read his own diaries—he's lost again, you know. Now, while it's still night and you are still strong, go fetch the machine and carry it to the palace. We'll meet you there."

CHAPTER TWENTY-SEVEN

Uncle Bill decided to help us carry the time-and-space machine to Buckingham Palace.

"We'll take my carriage to where you left it," he offered. "Tell my driver where to go, nephew."

"We're going home, we're going home." Lucy sang a little song to herself.

"Tell him, Mr. Talbot," Ralf Alfa encouraged as he swung himself to the roof of the carriage.

Mr. Talbot was silent.

"Uh oh," said Oliver Twit. "You were lost when we met. You have no idea where you left the thinga-majig, right, guv?"

"I'm thinking. I'm thinking. There were streetlights. All the buildings were no more than four stories high."

"There were outhouses in all of the backyards," Lucy added.

"And some had small stables," Billy Furball said.

"That could be almost anywhere in London," Oliver Twit said. "Didn't you see any landmarks on the street—a big building like a church or a park or a street sign or . . ."

"There was a store on the corner of the street. It had a funny name . . . ," I said. "I can't . . . oh yes, The Something and Something . . ."

"Oh, big help, Norman," Lucy Fang snarled.

"Sounds like it could be a pub," said Oliver Twit. "Anyone else remember it?"

"Wait! Wait! It had a funny cutout sign in the shape of . . . of . . ." Billy Furball had closed his eyes and was drooling.

"It's making him hungry—the sign must be of something edible," Lucy said.

"Or something that could be eaten if cooked," I said. "Like an animal. Or a vegetable or . . . wait. I remember. It was a chop, like a giant pork chop. It hung below the name. Which was . . ."

"The Chop and Chip," we all remembered at once.

"My old neighborhood," said Oliver Twit. "Got some succulent handouts from that pub—meaty bones to gnaw on, chips that were not too soggy . . ."

"Lead the way, my boy," Uncle Bill said. "You sit with the driver. The rest of you squeeze inside. Can't go racing through London as werewolves. Are you joining us, Mr. Holmes?"

"It seems my services are no longer of any importance," Sherlock Holmes complained.

"Nonsense. Since we must keep concealed, would you mind riding on top with Oliver and the driver? You, too, Dr. Watson."

The overloaded carriage took off into the dark London night.

CHAPTER TWENTY-EIGHT

Henry finally proved useful. We couldn't remember exactly what roof we wanted, so he flew up and down the street and spotted the time-and-space machine. We climbed up the side of the building.

"Someone's hung laundry all over it."

"Any parts missing?"

"How should I know?"

"How do we get it down from here?"

"Brute force."

We folded the laundry and put the heavy machine on the edge of the roof. Then we made a werewolf chain down the side of the building and slid the machine from wolf to wolf. Mr. Talbot was in the street. He was going to catch it but became kind of a werewolf safety net instead.

"It fell on his head."

"Is he alive?"

"Can't tell. He's under it. No. Yes. His feet are moving!"

"I'm fine. Just get this off of me."

We decided that the best and fastest way to get the time-and-space machine to Buckingham Palace was to put it on top of the carriage.

"You werewolves will have to run alongside. The wheels are barely holding up now." Sherlock Holmes took charge.

"We'll be spotted," said Lucy Fang.

"It's four o'clock in the morning. Few people will see you, and no one will believe their accounts of wolflike creatures escorting a carriage," Sherlock Holmes insisted.

"We had better get a move on," Mr. Talbot said.

"Are you too squashed to run?"

"Not quite."

CHAPTER TWENTY-NINE

When we arrived at Buckingham Palace, we were escorted through a side gate. Mrs. Talbot was waiting for us in a courtyard in front of a stable.

"Take that thing off the carriage and get rid of the old batteries. Fast. Then put these in. *Don't* mix them up. And don't put the new ones in upside down."

She handed us three shopping bags filled with double-A batteries. The sky was getting a little lighter. I could feel my werewolf powers fading. We took turns carefully inserting the 212 batteries. By the time we finished, the werewolves were just a bunch of kids and two adults standing around in torn clothing.

"Your lovely shoes. What a pity," said Oliver Twit.

"When we remember, we take them off before we go running."

"Where's the queen?" asked Billy Furball.

"What's it to you?" said Oliver Twit.

"I think I liked her, that's all."

"She's asleep in her own bed as we all should be. Now help me," Mrs. Talbot said, pointing to the stable.

We opened the stable doors and saw a shining metal machine. It was sleek. It was modern. It had buttons and dials and small computer screens. And two seats. I think we were counting on riding home with Mrs. Talbot and not in the old prototype.

"Who gets to go with you?" Lucy Fang asked.

"All of you. Do you think I'd let you wander around that gray in-between place in that old thing? I'm going to tow you."

"Tow?"

"Tow. Now help me secure this rope and we'll be off."

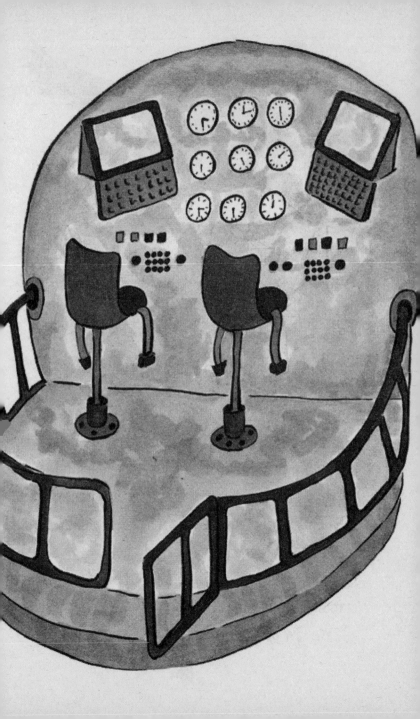

CHAPTER THIRTY

We probably tied more knots than were necessary, but we didn't want to take the chance of being set adrift—again.

We said good-bye to Mr. Holmes and Dr. Watson, hugged and thanked Uncle Bill, Lord William Talbot, and told Oliver Twit we'd really miss him. Mr. Talbot had a private last-minute talk with Uncle Bill and we climbed into the old time-and-space machine. Mrs. Talbot gave orders to Mr. Talbot, who fiddled with the controls of the prototype while she punched buttons and twisted dials of her machine.

"Ten steps back now!" she barked at the people standing around the machines.

We saw people moving away from us into the gray

morning and then, as the time-and-space machine started to shake, Oliver Twit leaped in next to me.

"What are you doing?" I asked.

"Not much for me in London, is there?" he said. "I thought I'd have a look at the future."

We were in the gray foggy place once more. No one could see anything.

"Who's that with you? Did Oliver Twit get into this machine?"

"I did."

"What are you going to do in the twenty-first century? You can't be a pickpocket and beggar. How will you live?"

"By my wits, like always."

"Why did you do it? Why come with us?"

"For the shoes, of course."

"He's kidding, isn't he?"

"Possibly not."

Suddenly the air around us cleared. The machine bumped along the ground. We looked up. The sky was dark and clear and filled with stars.

"Cor, that's beautiful," said Oliver Twit taking a

deep breath. "Can I live here?"

"Almost. You'll come home with me for now," said Mrs. Talbot. "Climb on next to me. As for the rest of you, this is the same night you left. Your parents think you are on a backyard campout following some wolf fun. Don't go home till morning."

"I'm confused," said Ralf Alfa.

"Do we have to sleep outside, Mr. Talbot?" I asked.

"There's plenty of floor space and lots of blankets inside."

"Good night, son," said Mrs. Talbot as she and Oliver Twit and the two time machines disappeared into thin air.

"She towed my machine away," Mr. Talbot whined as he led us into the house.

"One of our better adventures, don't you think?" Lucy Fang asked.

"There is one thing I don't understand," Ralf Alfa said. "I can understand that Sherlock Holmes knew all about werewolves—as a detective he knew all kinds of odd things. But Queen Victoria seemed comfortable with the idea, and that surprised me."

"I can explain that," Mr. Talbot said. "Uncle Bill told me just before we left. Her late husband, Prince Albert? You know about him?"

"Yes," we answered. "What about him?"

"Werewolf," Mr. Talbot said.

"Oh," we all said.

END

3 1143 00979 7367